ASK EVA

JUDI CURTIN grew up in Cork and now lives in Limerick where she is married with three children. Judi is the author of *Eva's Journey*, *Eva's Holiday* and *Leave it to Eva*, as well as the best-selling 'Alice & Megan' series. With Roisin Meaney, she is the author of *See If I Care*. She has also written three novels, *Sorry, Walter*, *From Claire to Here* and *Almost Perfect*. Her books have been translated into many languages and sold around the world.

Judi Curtin

ASK EVA

THE O'BRIEN PRESS
DUBLIN

For Dan, Brian, Ellen and Annie.

First published 2013 by The O'Brien Press Ltd,
12 Terenure Road East, Rathgar, Dublin 6, Ireland.
Tel: +353 1 4923333; Fax: +353 1 4922777
E-mail: books@obrien.ie
Website: www.obrien.ie

ISBN: 978-1-84717-544-1

A catalogue record for this title is available from the British Library

1 2 3 4 5 6 7 8
13 14 15 16

Layout and design: The O'Brien Press Ltd
Cover illustration: Woody Fox
Printed and bound by CPI Group (UK) Ltd, Croydon, CR0 4YY
The paper used in this book is produced using pulp from managed forests

The O'Brien Press receives assistance from

Joey

Chapter One

'Why don't you ask Eva?'

'Ask me what?' I said, dropping my schoolbag onto the kitchen table where my mum and her friend Monica were drinking tea and chatting.

Mum smiled at me, 'I was just saying that Monica should ask you to find out what's wrong with Joey.'

'Why?' I asked. 'Is he sick?'

Monica shook her head, 'No, not sick exactly, but he's not his normal cheerful self these days either.'

Joey is Monica's son, who's eight. He often stays with us, and sometimes he even comes on our holidays. He's kind of like the little brother I never had. He's always laughing and whistling, and I'd never, ever seen him in a bad mood.

'I'm guessing you've tried asking him what's wrong?' I said.

Monica sighed, 'I've asked him a hundred times, but he just says he's fine and then changes the subject as quickly as possible. I have to go to hospital next week, and I can't stop worrying about him.'

'You're going to hospital?' I said grinning. 'That's *great* news.'

'Eva!' said Mum, and I realised what

I'd said.

'Ooops,' I said. 'Sorry to hear you're going to hospital, Monica. What I meant is, I'm glad Joey will be coming to stay with us. He always brightens the place up.'

'He's looking forward to it too,' said Monica. 'And maybe, while he's here, you could find out what's bothering him.'

'Sure I will,' I said. 'Just leave it to me.'

When I got home from school a few days later, Joey was in the living room. The TV was on, but he wasn't watching it. He was just sitting there, pulling at the cuff of his school jumper.

'Hey,' I said. 'You're here! That's great. How are things?'

'Fine,' he muttered, with a face that was saying the opposite.

'You must be worried about your mum's operation.'

He shook his head, 'Not really. It's only a little operation this time, and Mum's hoping it's going to be the last one. Anyway, she'll be home in a few days.'

Now I was all out of ideas. Joey was still pulling at the cuff of his jumper, and it was starting to unravel. I'd never seen him sit in the same place for so long.

I decided to go for the direct approach.

'Are you worried about something, Joey?' I asked.

Now when he looked at me, his eyes seemed huge and unhappy.

'No,' he said.

I didn't believe him for a second.

'You can tell me if you are,' I said. 'You can tell me anything at all.'

'Everything's fine,' he said. 'Just fine.'

As soon as I'd finished my homework, I went back into the living room. Joey was still there, still not watching the TV. He'd unravelled half the cuff of his jumper, and was chewing the curly wool.

'How about a game of Monopoly?'

I asked. (I think Monopoly is the most boring game in the history of the universe, but Joey loves it, so I thought my offer would cheer him up.)

He didn't even look up.

'No, thanks,' he said.

'Why don't I walk you over to the green near your house? You can join in a soccer game with the boys from your road for a while. There's time before tea. We could ......'

I stopped talking when I noticed that Joey's heel was tapping furiously against the leg of the couch. He gave a sudden pull on the sodden thread and ripped the sleeve of his jumper almost up to the elbow.

'I don't want to go there,' he

whispered.

'Hey, Joey,' I said. 'What's wrong? You always play soccer with those boys. You're one of the best players there. They're your friends.'

He shook his head. 'No they're not. I hate them. I hate them all.'

'It's OK,' I said. 'Let's not go today. We can go tomorrow instead.'

Joey stared at me like I was threatening to cut off his fingers one by one.

'*No!*' he said. 'I'm not playing with them any more. Ever.'

He looked both angry and sad – not a good combination.

I gave him a hug.

'Whatever,' I said. 'Let's just watch

TV for a while.'

So I sat down beside him, and for a long time we watched TV and pretended that everything was fine.

Later I told Mum about our conversation.

'You clever girl,' she said. 'I knew you'd find out what was going on.'

I sighed, 'All I know is that it's got something to do with the boys who live near Joey. Even if I find out exactly what that is, there's still the small detail of what I'm going to do about it.'

Mum hugged me.

'I have great faith in you,' she said. 'I know you'll figure it out.'

Chapter Two

Next day, while I was still trying to decide how to help Joey, my friend Ella came over. We went up to my room and I told her the whole story.

When we came downstairs ten minutes later, we were ready for the first part of our plan – finding out what was going on with Joey and his 'friends'.

'Hey Joey,' I said as Ella and I walked into the living room. 'We're going for a walk. Want to come?'

He shook his head. 'No, thanks.'

'We're buying ice-creams,' I said.

That made Joey look up and smile! It's kind of sad how easy it is to bribe little boys with the promise of ice-cream.

'OK,' he said. 'Can I get a chocolate one?'

I grinned. 'Of course you can. You can have any one you want.'

Joey followed us, and looked puzzled as Ella and I turned left outside our garden gate.

'Isn't the shop the other way?' he asked.

'There's a bigger shop this way,' explained Ella. 'That's where the best ice-creams are.'

Joey didn't say anything else until we came close to the street where he lives. Then he began to drag his feet and lag behind.

'Oh, look, Joey,' I said, pretending I'd forgotten our conversation from the day before. 'Your friends are playing football. Why don't you join in for a while? Ella and I don't mind waiting.'

Joey had a panicked look on his face and I was feeling really sorry for him, when one of the boys saw us and ran over.

'Hey, Joey,' he said.

'Hey, Luke,' said Joey.

'Do you want to play?' asked Luke.

Joey was starting to smile when a bigger boy picked up the ball and ran over.

'You can't play, Joey,' he said. 'We've picked teams already and you're not on one.'

'But—' began Luke, but the bigger boy pushed him away. 'You're in goals, Luke,' he said. 'And if you don't go over now, you won't be able to play either.'

Luke hesitated for a second, like he was trying to decide what to do. Then, with an embarrassed smile, he walked away to stand between the two jumpers on the far side of the green.

'So long, Loser Baby Joey,' said the bigger boy.

I know that violence is wrong, but I really, really felt like thumping him. I took a step forward, but Ella pulled me back.

'*Not* a good idea,' she said, reading my mind.

The boy was still standing there.

'Come on, guys,' I said, putting my arms around Ella and Joey. 'We're out of here. So long Loser … Loser whatever your name is.'

It was totally pathetic, and I couldn't blame the boy for laughing at me. He ran off and the game began again.

'OMG,' I said, as we walked away. 'Do you want me to sort that boy out for you, Joey?'

He shook his head. 'No. He'd only be nice to me until you're gone, and then ……'

He was rubbing his eyes furiously, trying to hide the tears that were welling up. His bottom lip began to wobble. I desperately wanted to hug him, but I was afraid the boys would laugh at him if I did.

'Who is he anyway?' I asked.

'That's Rhys,' he said. 'He moved here a few weeks ago. He's not very nice.'

'I can see that,' said Ella.

'Does he ever let you play?' I asked.

'You can only play if you're in his gang,' said Joey.

'And you're not in his gang?' asked Ella.

Once more Joey shook his head, 'Rhys says I'm a baby, and babies can't be in his gang.'

'Why does he say that?' I asked.

Joey's face went red. 'The last time I was going to stay at your place, I was carrying my stuff out to the car and Rhys saw my teddy.'

'Buster?' I asked, thinking of the totally cute green teddy who always sleeps on the end of Joey's bed.

Joey nodded, 'Yeah. When Rhys saw him, he started calling me a baby, and after that he wouldn't let me play soccer.'

'That's totally mean,' I said. 'There's nothing wrong with having a teddy. I bet even Rhys has one.'

'He hasn't,' said Joey. 'He said he gave all of his away when he was two.'

'How come the other boys play with him when he's so mean?' asked Ella.

Joey shrugged. 'I think they're afraid of him. I'm kind of afraid of him too.'

'So why didn't you tell your mum?' I asked.

'I didn't want to make her sad,' he said.

Now we were far enough away that I could risk giving him a little hug.

'Don't worry,' I said. 'You've told me now. I'll sort all this out.'

'How?' asked Joey, staring at me with his huge eyes.

'Er … I haven't worked out all the finer details yet,' I said. 'But when I'm finished with Rhys, he's going to be very nice to you – very nice indeed!'

At the shop, Ella and I bought Joey a huge ice-cream and a packet of crisps and two bars of chocolate.

'Thanks,' he said.

He smiled for a second, but the smile faded quickly. Some things can't be fixed with food.

Next day, Ella called over.

'I have an idea,' she said.

'You have no idea how glad I am to hear those words,' I sighed. 'I spent the whole night racking my brain, but all the ideas that came to me were either totally stupid, totally impossible or totally illegal.'

Ella grinned. 'Well, you know my mum's friend, Doreen?' I shook my head, and Ella continued, 'Anyway, that's not important. What's important is that Doreen's son is Bradley Buckley, and.....'

I grabbed her arm. '*The* Bradley

Buckley?'

She nodded, 'Yeah, that's the one. Anyway, Bradley's really nice and—'

Now I squeezed her arm harder. 'You actually *know* Bradley Buckley, the star of the local soccer team? How come you never told me that?'

She smiled sweetly. 'You never asked me. Anyway, as I was saying, Bradley's really nice, so I was thinking, we could bring him to meet Joey, and then Joey mightn't feel so bad about Rhys, and—'

By now my fingers were hurting from squeezing her arm. 'That's a great idea, Ella,' I said. 'And I know how to make it even better.'

Chapter Three

At lunch-time the next day, four of us went to the green near Joey's house – Joey, Bradley, Ella and me.

'Oh no! There's no one here,' I said, disappointed.

'They're probably all gone for their lunch,' said Joey. 'That's not a problem. When they come back, we'll be ready for them.'

I grinned. Already he was sounding like the brave and funny boy he was supposed to be.

By the time Rhys and the other

boys appeared, Joey and Bradley were kicking a ball to each other. Bradley had his hood up, and a scarf covering most of his face, so no-one recognised him.

When Rhys saw the two teddies sitting on a rug, propped up against Joey's gear-bag, his face lit up. It's easy to make a bully happy.

'Ha, ha,' he said to Joey. 'You've got two teddies now – that makes you a Double Loser Baby.'

Bradley stopped kicking the ball, and walked towards Rhys.

'Only one of those teddies belongs to Joey,' he said. 'The other one is mine. He's called Marbles. I bring him everywhere with me. He's my lucky mascot.'

Rhys was starting to laugh, when Bradley slowly unwound his scarf and pulled down his hood.

Rhys stopped laughing. His face went pale and he took a little step backwards.

'You're …' he began, '… you're …' He couldn't finish.

Bradley bent down and picked up his teddy and cuddled it.

'I'm a man who loves his teddy,' he said.

Suddenly all the other boys recognised Bradley and they ran at him in a loud, excited little-boy rush.

'OMG, you're Bradley Buckley!'

'Can I get my mum to take a picture of you with me?'

'Can I have your autograph?'

'Will you play soccer with us?'

Bradley grinned at them, 'Yes,' he said. 'Let's play soccer.'

By now, Rhys had recovered. He pushed his way forward and grabbed the ball from one of the other boys.

'Let's get started, lads,' he said. 'I'm captain of one team, and I'm going to be centre forward. You can be on my team, Bradley.'

Bradley leaned forward and took the ball from him.

'Not so fast,' he said. 'I'm making the rules today, and the first rule is that everyone needs to go home and get their teddy. All the teddies can sit here together and keep Marbles and Buster company.'

The boys stood and looked at him, not really understanding what was going on.

'That's stupid,' said Rhys.

Bradley shrugged. 'Maybe,' he said. 'But it's the rule. So what's everyone waiting for?'

There was a sudden scuffle as most of the boys raced home. Soon only Rhys and Joey and another small boy were left. The small boy looked ready to cry.

'I haven't got a teddy,' he said. 'I've only got a bunny. Can I bring him instead?'

Bradley patted his shoulder gently, 'Of course you can.'

The boy beamed and ran off home.

'What about you?' asked Bradley,

turning to Rhys, who was turning out to be tougher than I'd expected.

'Only babies play with teddies,' he muttered.

Rhys held out for a long time.

He held out while the other boys came racing back from home carrying an assorment of big and small and dirty and clean teddies (and a bunny) and lined them up on the rug. He held out while Joey and Luke picked teams, and the boys lined up excitedly in their positions.

But when Bradley was placing the ball in the middle of the pitch for the start of the game, Rhys couldn't hold out any more.

He ran over to Bradley, and tugged his hoodie.

'I think I might have a teddy at home somewhere,' he said.

Bradley grinned at Ella and me, and then he turned back to Rhys. 'So, go get it,' he said. 'We'll wait for you.'

A few minutes later, Rhys was back with a very old, very worn teddy under his arm.

'Looks well-loved,' said Ella giggling.

Everyone watched as Rhys lined his teddy up on the rug with the others.

'What's your teddy called?' asked Bradley.

Rhys went red, 'Er … er … he's called … er … James Bond,' he said.

Bradley narrowed his eyes.

'Not sure I believe you,' he said.

Now Rhys went even redder.

'It's Teddy Weddy,' he whispered.

For one tiny second I actually felt sorry for him.

Bradley smiled. 'Cool name,' he said. 'Now you go over there and join Luke's team, and let's get started.'

When the match was over, I watched as Rhys went over to Joey.

'You can be in my gang if you want,' he said.

'I don't want to be in your gang,' said Joey bravely. 'I just want to play soccer. Can I play with you tomorrow?'

Rhys nodded.

'Can I play the next day?'

Rhys nodded again.

'And will you bring Teddy Weddy to watch?'

Rhys hesitated, and I wondered if Joey had gone too far. But Rhys put his head down. 'Maybe,' he said.

Bradley, Ella and Joey all had tea at my place that evening. Marbles and Buster sat together at the end of the table.

'It was so kind of you to help Joey like that, Bradley,' said Mum.

'Yeah,' said Dad. 'Pretending to love your teddy like that was genius.'

'Who said I was pretending?' asked

Bradley, as he picked up Marbles and stroked his head gently.

He had a funny twinkle in his eye. I couldn't tell if he was joking or not, but that didn't seem important.

Joey picked up Buster, and the two teddies gave each other high fives. It wasn't amazingly funny, but even so, we all laughed for a long time, and Joey laughed loudest of all.

Dawn

Chapter One

'There's Dawn,' said Ella, pointing at a figure sitting in a parked car a few streets away from our school. 'Oh! … it looks like she's crying.'

We walked a bit closer, and I could see that Ella was right. It was Dawn, a really nice classroom assistant from our school. She was hunched over the steering wheel, sobbing, and rubbing her eyes with a soggy-looking tissue.

'OMG,' I said. 'I wonder what's wrong with her.'

'Should we go over and ask?' said Ella.

I didn't know the answer to that. It

was kind of weird and embarrassing seeing a grown-up cry. Just then Dawn looked up, and when she saw us, she quickly turned away. Even though I felt sorry for her, I knew it was best to pretend we hadn't spotted her.

As soon as Ella and I got to the school hallway, we saw a huge crowd of kids gathered around the noticeboard. Everyone was laughing.

We pushed through the crowd and made a space for ourselves in front of the notice-board. Everyone was staring at a page pinned right in the centre – it was pink, with little hand-drawn hearts all around the edge. On the top it said 'Dawn's Poetic Diary' in curly letters. I knew the right thing to do was to grab the page and rip it up, but it was like when there's something really scary on TV – you don't want to look, and yet you can't help yourself.

I 've met the only man I will ever love,
He is a treasure, sent from above,
Of my heart he has taken a sliver,
When I see him I always shiver,
But he does not know how I feel
And so my poor heart will never heal,
Of my poem this is the gist –
My true love barely knows that I exist

'OMG,' I whispered to Ella as soon as I'd finished reading.

'OMG, is right,' she said. 'That is really, really bad poetry.'

'That's not why I said OMG,' I said. 'Not everyone can be a Shakespeare, but poetry like that is private. It's not meant to be read by anyone except the writer.'

'Maybe Dawn didn't write this,' she whispered back. 'Maybe someone just made it up to embarrass her.'

I shook my head.

'I've seen Dawn writing in a notebook with paper like this, and besides, if it wasn't her diary, she wouldn't be sitting in her car crying like she'd just been voted off the *X-Factor*.'

Before I could decide what to do, Mrs Parker, our totally scary principal, came along. She didn't have to push through the crowd, it sort of dissolved at her touch as everyone slithered away.

Ella and I watched as Mrs Parker ripped the pink page from the notice-board. She tore it into four neat pieces, which she crumpled up and threw into the recycling bag next to the side door.

'That's the end of that,' she said.

Only it wasn't.

At lunch-time, there was another group of kids gathered at the door to the boys toilets. Before I got there, I knew what I was going to see.

Once again it was a pink page, with Dawn's Poetic Diary writen on the top. This time the edge was decorated with tiny bluebirds.

I see him every single day
I want to sing like a lark in May
When he smiles with his big brown eyes
He makes the ship of my heart capsize
How long more can I stand the pain?
When will I dare to write his name?

Underneath, in a different pen, and untidy block capitals, were the words – 'KEEP WATCHING. THIS STORY IS GOING TO RUN ALL WEEK!'

'OMG,' I said to Ella. 'She sees him every morning. Who can he be? Do you think he works near here?'

'Maybe he actually works here,' said Ella. 'Maybe he's one of the teachers.'

Suddenly I realised why Dawn was so very upset. Whoever had stolen or found her diary was enjoying releasing it in little bits. Dawn was the only one who knew what was coming next.

A teacher appeared. 'Clear off, you lot,' he said, before taking the page and ripping it up.

'There's more,' I said to Ella as we walked away with all the other kids. 'I bet there's more, and I bet it's worse. Poor, poor Dawn.'

When we were lined up and waiting to go back to our classes, Mrs Parker and all the other teachers and teaching assistants, except for Dawn, appeared. Mrs Parker gave a big, long, vague speech about honesty and respect and privacy. She didn't mention Dawn's diary, but she didn't need to – everyone knew what she was talking about.

I stopped listening after a while. I couldn't help looking at all the male teachers, trying to see which ones had brown eyes. Most of the ones who did were married, or old or both. I was kind of relieved to see that Ella's dad – who teaches in our school – had dark grey eyes.

'Do you think it'll stop now that Mrs P has given us a lecture?' asked Ella as we went back to class.

I shook my head. 'Some of the kids in the higher classes aren't afraid of Mrs Parker. And whoever's doing this is having too much fun to stop. They're going to go on with this until every single page of Dawn's diary has been revealed.'

'You're right,' said Ella. 'This is going to get a whole lot worse before it gets better. Maybe we should get all our friends to patrol the corridors, ripping these down before anyone else sees them.'

I shook my head. 'That's a good idea, but it's too late now that everyone has seen the poems. The only way to help Dawn is to make people forget about her and her secret, brown-eyed love.'

'How are we going to do that?'

'I don't know,' I said. 'But we're going to have to think of something.'

At home-time, no one was surprised to see a pink page stuck to the back gate of the school.

My darling, darling, darling boy.
Please don't treat me like a toy
The only thing my poor heart misses
Is the sweet warmth of your kisses
Without you, nothing can I enjoy,
Ask me out and don't be coy.
If you don't, I'll surely die
Please, please, please, listen to my cry.

Underneath it said – 'NEXT INSTALMENT TOMORROW!'

Ella made a face.

'I think we'd better think a bit faster, Eva,' she said, and I knew she was right.

Chapter Two

Next morning Ella and I got to school early, even though I was tired. I'd been up very late the night before, e-mailing my ideas to Ella, and laughing at the ones she e-mailed back. It was after two o'clock in the morning by the time we were finished.

Ella was nervous.

'We could get into a whole lot of trouble for this,' she said. 'Did I ever tell you that I'm really, really afraid of Mrs Parker?'

'Don't worry about her,' I said. 'She wouldn't hurt a fly.'

'That's just because no fly would ever dare to buzz around her head annoying her.'

I giggled, trying to sound more confident than I felt.

'Be brave,' I said. 'We're doing this for Dawn. Now here's your sellotape. Let's get to work.'

By the time the other kids arrived, there were pink pages stuck to almost every wall of the school. They were all handwritten. They were all decorated with little pictures at the edges. They all rhymed – sort of. They were all very, very embarrassing for the teachers who had 'written' them. There was almost a riot as kids rushed from one to another, trying to read them all.

Ella hugged me.

'That was a totally, totally genius idea, Eva,' she said. 'Now everyone will think that Dawn's pages were made up too. Even if someone sticks up the rest of them, no one will care.'

So that people wouldn't suspect that it was us, we stopped at a poem, and read it out. It was the one that Ella had written about Mr Gowing.

'He's my dad,' she'd said. 'It's only fair that I should be the one who gets to mock him.'

It was called 'Mr Gowing's One True Love':

My one true love is maths
I love it more than hot baths

Graphs make my heart rate soar
Numbers shake my very core
Geometry turns me on
Algebra is so much fun
Sometimes I wish I was single
As maths makes my whole body tingle

Mrs Parker came out of her office when she heard all the noise.

'What on earth is going on here?' she asked.

Everyone acted like they couldn't hear her as they pretended to be really keen to get to their classes on time. Ella and I backed away and watched in horror as Mrs Parker stopped at the worst poem of all, the one I'd called 'Mrs Parker's Sweetheart.'

Ella and I peeped around a corner, and we watched as Mrs Parker fumbled around in her pocket for her glasses.

'Maybe we shouldn't have done this,' I whispered, trying to hide the shaking in my voice.

'Maybe Mrs Parker's got a sense of humour,' said Ella.

'And maybe pigs will fly,' I said. 'Face it, Ella, if we're found out, we're both dead.'

By now Mrs Parker had located her glasses. She leaned forward and stared at the page. Ella gripped my arm tightly as we watched the very scary principal silently read the words I'd written:

I love my dear husband with all of my heart

I love him more than apple tart
I love him more than that Simpson boy, Bart,
I love him because he's very smart
I love him so much I can almost forgive him
when he does a super-duper-stinky fart.

I was still holding my breath when Mrs Parker slowly reached up and took down the page. She crumpled it in her hand, and walked past us, back into her office. Her face was red. She did not look happy.

'You're right as usual,' said Ella. 'If Mrs Parker finds out that we're behind this, we are totally, totally dead.'

I saw Dawn a few times that morning.

She looked a bit pale, but not as sad as she had the day before. Kids weren't laughing at her any more – they were too busy repeating lines from the poems Ella and I had written.

After lunch, I was almost beginning to relax, when there was a loud knock on the classroom door. Mrs Parker walked in.

'Excuse me, for interrupting,' she said, smiling sweetly at our teacher. Then she turned around and snapped, 'Eva Gordon and Ella Gowing. My office. Now.'

Everyone stared as Ella and I got up and followed Mrs Parker. As we walked along the corridor, I could see that Ella was shaking. I wanted to comfort her, but didn't know how – and besides, I was shaking a bit myself.

In the office, Mrs Parker sat down, and Ella and I stood facing her, across the huge desk. I hadn't been inside that room since the day I'd started in the school. It sooo wasn't a place I wanted to be.

'It has come to my attention that the recent spate of disrespectful "poetry" in our corridors is your work,' said Mrs Parker. 'Would either of you like to comment?'

I was tempted to ask how she knew, but didn't trust myself to say anything without bursting into tears, so I shook my head, and Ella did the same.

Mrs Parker launched into the same

speech about respect and privacy that she'd given the day before. I wondered if she'd learned it off by heart in teacher training college. Had she waited thirty years for this occasion, just so she could dust down the boring old words and use them again?

'I will of course be writing to your parents,' she said in the end. 'The fact that I won't even have to post your letter, Ella, that I can just hand it to your father in the staff-room, that makes things even worse.'

I glanced at Ella and saw tears in her eyes. Her dad gets mad at her if she does anything wrong at school. Suddenly I felt really bad. What was the point of trying to help Dawn, if it also got my friend into huge trouble?

'It was only me,' I said suddenly. 'Ella didn't have anything to do with it.'

Ella rubbed a tear from her cheek with the sleeve of her jumper. 'It was both of us,' she whispered.

Just then there was a knock on the door.

'I'm busy,' called Mrs Parker, but the door opened anyway, and Dawn stepped into the room. She didn't look at Ella or me.

'There's something I have to say, Mrs Parker,' she said. 'It's very important. It's about those pages that have been appearing around the school.'

Mrs Parker stared at her. 'I'm listening,' she said.

Now Dawn spoke in a rush. 'I'm the one who wrote those poems. I'm the one who stuck them up.'

Mrs Parker's voice was like nails on a blackboard. 'These two girls have already admitted to doing that.'

'They're saying that so I won't get into trouble,' said Dawn. 'But I can't let them take the blame. I can't stand by and watch them suffer for something I did.'

Mrs Parker narrowed her eyes and glared at Dawn.

'Some of those verses are about you,' she said. 'Do you expect me to believe that you wrote stupid lines about yourself and displayed them on the notice-board for all the world to see? Why would you do such a thing? And if you would do such a thing, how could you expect to be allowed to keep your job?'

I gasped. Had I made things even worse for Dawn too? Had I made a huge mess of everything?

Dawn didn't answer, and Mrs Parker continued to speak. 'And once you'd finished flaunting your own love life, you moved on to write scurrilous poems about other staff members. I was an English teacher for three decades, and I've never before seen a single writer produce work in such different styles. The first poems were about you, Dawn, and they were intense and personal, and the second ones were rather pathetic and childish ...'

How dare Mrs Parker diss our works

of art like that? Ella and I had stayed up half the night writing them. But this wasn't about us any more.

Now Mrs Parker stopped talking for a second. She stared into space and then a funny look came over her face, like she was just working things out.

Finally she gave a big long sigh. 'I'm not sure I'm ever going to get to the bottom of this. Maybe we can only hope that everyone has learned a valuable lesson. Maybe those letters to your parents will be unnecessary, after all.'

Then something amazing happened. For the tiniest of seconds, a smile fluttered across Mrs Parker's face, as she glanced at my crumpled-up poem, which was still on her desk.

'I don't like apple tart all that much,' she said, almost to herself. 'Blueberry tart would have been more apt.'

I couldn't meet her eye.

Had Mrs Parker just figured out what had really happened?

Did she know exactly when Ella and I had got involved, and why?

Did she actually have a sense of humour?

I looked out the window, half-expecting to see a huge pink pig sailing through the air.

A few days later, the whole thing was forgotten. After one boy had been given detention for reciting my poem about Mrs Parker, no one else dared to do the same. No more pages of 'Dawn's Poetic Diary' had appeared and kids had stopped laughing at her. I figured that whoever had got their hands on her book had decided not to share any more of it.

Then, on Friday, a teacher sent me on a message to the caretaker. On the way, I passed Dawn, who was checking off the milk delivery. She was smiling at the delivery man, and he was smiling back at her – with huge brown eyes!! I was so excited I could hardly think. I raced to the caretaker's office, gave my message, and then I raced back to the hall. Luckily, the delivery man was still carrying in crates of milk. I rushed over, pretending to hold the door for him.

'Oh,' I nearly forgot,' I said loudly to Dawn. 'My teacher gave me a message for you too.'

'What is it?' asked Dawn. She wasn't looking at me. She was still gazing lovingly at the delivery man who was now stacking the milk crates against the wall.

'It's to do with the film you were talking about,' I said. 'The one you are both dying to see.'

'What film?' I couldn't blame Dawn for looking puzzled, since I'd just invented a conversation between her and my teacher, who weren't even that friendly.

'The one you were both going to see tomorrow night,' I said. 'Only now my teacher can't go after all. She'd hate the tickets to go to waste. She hopes you'll be able to find someone else to go with.'

Dawn was going red, but she wasn't giving me the look that adults sometimes give kids – the silent one that says, 'Shut up now, or you're dead.' So I continued, 'I wonder who you could go with at such short notice?'

The delivery man had torn off the docket, and was holding it towards Dawn. He was looking at her with a soppy look. I have to admit, he was kind of cute, in a shy, not-very-confident kind of way. I had a horrible feeling that he would never, ever be brave enough to ask her out.

'Do you like going to the cinema?' I said to him.

Now he went as red as Dawn. 'Er …
yes … I do … actually … I …'

His voice trailed off and I sighed. Did
I have to do everything?

'Here's the deal,' I said, looking at
the two red-faced adults in front of me.
'Dawn has a spare ticket for the cinema.
You like going to the cinema. Can you
figure out the rest yourselves?'

Dawn looked at the delivery man,
and he looked back at her.

'Will you …?' he asked.

'Yes,' she said. 'I'd love to.'

I felt like patting them on the back,
but decided that was a step too far. So
I just said, 'Have fun,' and then I went
back to my lesson.

When Ella and I were walking home that afternoon, Dawn popped out from behind a hedge, almost like she'd been lying in wait for us.

'I need to say a big "thank you" to you two girls,' she said.

'That's OK,' said Ella and I together.

Dawn smiled a big soppy smile. 'I feel like this isn't really happening to me,' she said. 'I feel like I'm floating on air. I will never understand how the worst week of my life turned into the best week of my life.'

'I don't know either,' laughed Ella. 'Maybe you should ask Eva.'

Then Dawn gave us each a hug before she floated off into the sunset.

BOOKs rock!

Want to read more?

VISIT your local bookshop

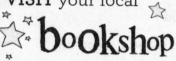

- ✔ Get great recommendations for books you'll love
- ✔ Meet your favourite authors & illustrators at brilliant events
- ✔ Discover books you never knew existed!

FIND YOUR LOCAL BOOKSHOP

www.booksellers.org.uk/bookshopsearch

JOIN your local library

You can browse and borrow from a huge selection of books and get recommendations of what to read next from expert librarians – all for FREE!

You can also discover libraries' wonderful children's and family reading activities – such as reading groups, author events and challenges (such as www.msreadathon.ie).

Get Online

Explore www.worldbookday.com to discover a world of bonkersly brilliant beautiful books!

- ✔ Downloads and activities for your favourite books and authors
- ✔ Cool games, trailers and videos
- ✔ Fantastic competitions
- ✔ Author events in your area
- ✔ Sign up for the FREE monthly e-newsletter

And much, much more...